The Great Downhill

❄ ❄ ❄

By Mitzi Harrisburg

Salt Water Media
29 Broad Street, Suite 104
Berlin, MD 21811
www.saltwatermedia.com

Cover image by David Klein and imaged used via
courtesy of www.unsplash.com

For additional copies, please visit bookshop.org.

This is a work of fiction. Many of the names, characters
and incidents in this book are used in a fictitious manner.
Any resemblance to actual persons, living or dead, or actual
events, is purely coincidental.

Dedication

This is my first book, dedicated to Mrs. F.,
who upon my graduation from high school,
asked me what I wanted to do with my life.
When I responded, "write a book," she laughed.

1

He was just another person on the bus — cool and aloof from the rest of the riders, nothing attractive enough to catch the eye. He was noticeable only because he was unknown. He wore a plaid jacket with a turtleneck sweater underneath, a beige colored one which didn't blend in with his skin. The others wore casual overalls and flannel farmers' shirts to keep them warm on the overnight bus trip. He had on corduroy bell-bottoms that ended up too short on his ankles, making his stained brown ankle boots more obvious than they should have been. And you could see his socks. His hair was streaked with gray and so was the mustache. He was a middle-aged man when I saw him, a little too unfriendly for me to perk up to. He was only another rider, someone who probably wanted to get away, who didn't join the crowd and have fun. He stuck to himself. Yet, occasionally, I'd notice a smile or a laugh. He was trying to be friendly. I remember saying to myself that he wasn't my type.

Ed, good ole' overweight Ed, brought the beer, and I helped him carry a single box of beer pretzels. He lugged his suitcase, the ring-baloney, and Ritz crackers. He thanked me for helping out "so much," and we climbed on-board. Kathy arrived late, in high, pre-ski spirits as always. *Ah, to be 23 again. To be naive and nice and oh so happy.* Kathy, who had thick luscious Italian hair and a small body frame, was new and buoyant like she got out of life everything she could. I was thinking that she must have been given this great built-in life survival kit that read, "LIFE IS WONDERFUL. LIFE IS GREAT. THINGS GO BETTER FOR KATHY." I somehow missed that injunction when it was given out.

Kathy and I shared twin seats and also shared food. She said she wasn't drinking that weekend, and I said to myself that I didn't want to drink either. I wanted to try myself out without that extra boost. I wanted to see how it went that weekend, with everything plus, on my own. No dependencies, no superficials, no booze. Just me.

I was tall and thin and was what they called "a dishwater blonde," with hair that was ashy or dark blonde with highlights. My skin was light, made darker by the sun in summer and a bronzer on my face in winter. My nose was full, not boney, and didn't have a bridge on it. Its shape made my face look balanced. My bones were big and my body angular, hidden only by the long sleeves and turtleneck sweaters that I wore all winter. My legs, in my opinion, were my best body part, kept muscular and thin by all the sports I played. My sister always laments that out of the four of Mom's 'girls', I got the biggest and roundest boobs.

A guy told me one time that "you're this side of

beautiful." It's amazing how make-up and a good hair day can transform 'ordinary' into 'almost beautiful'.

It was a good bus trip, perfect weather conditions, and a congenial driver. We left on a Thursday night from the suburbs of north New Jersey. Everyone of us worked the 9-to-5, and taking off for a long weekend of skiing was our thing. Ed asked me to sit with him, which I did for a while, until I realized that I had nothing to say to him for any length of time. He was out after every gal, and somehow, I found no security in his flirtations. He ended up calling me too conservative, at which point I buckled and cowered and feigned a karate chop right at the neck. I was trying to show him I wasn't conservative; but later on I figured if I am, then I am, and who the hell was I trying to impress anyway. I just wanted to be me, but I found no comfort in being "me." If he had said, "You're too wild," that would have stung too. Any criticism stung, and I always took it deeply and personally, just what the therapists tell us not to do. I wanted to hear, "You're the sexiest girl on the bus," but no such words came from Ed's lips. Not that he mattered much, because he was not sexy at all, and he was drinking, and somehow when I didn't drink, I didn't have much to say to guys.

Friday morning at the start of the ski at Killington,

I was quiet. The slopes were icy, with only a few inches of thick packed snow to work on. After my morning lesson, I was paralleling, using my uphill poles every other turn and shifting my weight onto the downhill ski. I was skiing down slopes that novices were using, a few moguls here and there, spread apart enough that I could manage them all-right. I even had an eye for the instructor, who, par for the course for ski slopes, was young, tanned, tall and good-looking. He had a lisp which came out occasionally when he talked, and his teeth were artificially white; nonetheless, he was rugged. Later on in the morning, when I had perfected my stem christies a little more in line with what he taught us, I was exuberant. I found him over at the Swiss ski school at the bottom of the slope, and hollered out, "Steve, it worked! What you said worked! It IS easier!"

He grinned a little without effort, and told me he gets this all day from his former students, and I yelled over, now thinking I had some credibility as a beginner, "Good!"

I continued on with my skiing, took the chair lift to the top of Little Spruce Mountain, skied Ridge Rim, then Smuggler, all the way to the bottom of Rickey's Run. I did a few more stem christies that were perfectly balanced, and did some that were shaky and uneven too. I kept forgetting to shift my weight completely on the downhill ski, but, finally, when I remembered to shift the weight, and use the poles on turns, I got it down right and did some pretty good skiing for a novice.

It was a beautiful day by late morning, warm enough to be hot at the bottom of the slope after 20 minutes of downhill, but cold enough at the top to need all the extra layers of long johns, undershirts, sweaters, socks, scarves, gloves, and hats. I continued skiing alone to help myself concentrate on what I was doing. It was the best thing I could have done. Even though I made mistakes, I practiced down the beginners' slope until I was finally tired and broke for lunch. I took up with Kathy and Cindy, another exuberant young skier, later on at the top of Little Spruce, only this time, I had road-mapped the intermediate slopes and tried my new skills on Sterling. Kathy and Cindy were tired; and after one more lift to the top of Big Spruce Mountain, we skied down Sterling and quit early for the day.

We were all exhausted when we met at the Steubin for the après ski and saw a few who were already there: Igor, the Latvian; Bill, the part-German, part-Irish, red-faced divorcee; and John, the big, I-don't-know-who with the German accent and one eye that was slightly crossed. I sipped hot tea while they glowed on martinis, gluhwein, and 7&7s. I was proud of myself that I hadn't imbibed. Even though they were giddy, loud, and obviously more loosened up, I wasn't tempted. I had had a good day of skiing, and I kept telling myself that I was stronger than them because I didn't need a drink at the end of the day.

I even managed to get through dinner without one.

Despite my insecurities, one time I was voted best dressed woman at work. Of course, there were only about ten female employees in the building, half of them over 50. The other half were young engineers who couldn't care less about clothes and make-up. My boss's wife had given me all her designer wool suits that she outgrew and I learned how make-up, woolen suits with short skirts, and leather high heels can quickly catch men's eyes. I also learned how strenuous sports, like skiing, tennis, volleyball and biking can keep a young woman's body slender, and help tame a ravenous appetite.

By nighttime, I started with a whiskey and water at the Baggy Knees, an old Vermont barn converted to a restaurant up the road from our lodge. All who wanted to go had loaded onto the bus about two hours after dinner, waived good-byes to all who stayed at the lodge, especially to Bill, who had sprained both his knees and ankle on the slopes that day. Bill's leg was swollen; and since he hadn't been to a doctor that day, he thought he was mildly injured and that the swelling would go down by the next morning.

The Baggy Knees was crowded, and the music was frenzied. The musicians were hippie freaks who played and played all night until our bodies on the dance floor were like pulp from exhaustion. The music turned the crowd into a mild hysteria as it got louder and longer. It took us up to a fevered peak, then abruptly let us down at the end. After finishing two whiskeys and water, I was loose, but paradoxically ready to go back to the lodge to bed.

Ed complained the whole time about the hard rock music, but he still danced. After the first whiskey and water, I told Ed on the dance floor that he was too conservative, and he replied, "Only one side."

I asked him which side, and he turned his back to me. I asked him if I could dance with his liberal side. I was trying to be humorous. We had fun dancing, fooling around on the dance floor and acting crazy. It was mostly a younger crowd, but our ski club group was mixed in age so everyone fit in. Age didn't matter; what did matter was that one didn't get too hot or smoke too much or drink too much. I had already smoked too much, and I knew I had to stop at two drinks in order to keep some control. Somehow, I knew when to stop drinking. It didn't take more than one to help me relax, and that was all I was after with the booze.

It was snowing outside when we left at midnight. This raised our spirits even more for the next day's skiing. We all went to bed happy, and I slept like a ground hog in hibernation.

By early Saturday, I was ready for the slopes again.

We were with Rafe, the aloof one on the bus, who seemed friendly enough. Kathy, Cindy and I took the gondola to the top of Mount Mansfield, the highest mountain in Vermont. It was a surround sound of beauty. We got another eight inches of snow overnight, and it was still snowing at 9 a.m. I told them I was afraid because I might have forgotten how to ski. I always got shaky on the lifts. I had learned to look at lifts with a lot more respect: one time in Vermont, I watched the Sugarbush Mountain ski patrol hoisting ropes around the waists of stranded chairlift victims and working for two or three hours to free them and get them down to the bottom of the slope. I had respect for it. Make that fear. All I had to do was look down the mountain, measure with a glance how many yards we were from the snowy ground, and I got that queasy feeling. Apparently, I was the only one it bothered. *Don't look down,* I told myself. *Look up, look up at beautiful Mt. Mansfield, look at this neat red gondola with four people in it, look at your ski boots, look at Kathy with her long, black, straight, thick Italian hair, look at Rafe's mustache … listen to Cindy tell you it's OK … tell yourself how gutsy you are … think of all your friends who wouldn't dare try to conquer the top of that frighteningly huge mountain with only what YOU know. Yes, think about your guts, because if it's one thing you've got, girl,* I told myself, *it's guts.*

The snow was blizzard-like at the top of Mt. Mansfield — cold, windy, raw. Yet thermometers at the top of the lift said 40 degrees. Something was wrong somewhere. I was more than freezing. I was shaking: my knees, my legs, even my brain was wobbling inside my head. It wasn't the previous night's whiskey. No, it was more like the expert slopes ahead of me that I knew that I, the novice, now had to ski down.

Somehow, Rafe, Cindy, Igor, John, Kenny, Kathy, and I got down Perry Merrill slope by the strength of our ankles. We all fell, many times. The snow was powdered, and it had turned the novice Perry Merrill slope into an intermediate or expert slope. I asked myself what a beginner like myself was doing in a dangerous place like this. Every time I fell, my knees would wobble more, and I forced myself not to stop and not look down the rest of the slope. It was when I looked down that I got shaky, and I lost my guts when I saw the rest of my team falling down into twisted little bodies with poles, skis, and boots sticking up at odd angles out of the snow. But I kept reminding myself not to look down, just to pick myself up and start skiing again. And not to think about it, because if I did, I'd lose my courage, take off my skis, and walk down to the bottom of the mountain like I did that one time skiing with the club at Sugarbush.

I couldn't let myself give up again, as this time I'd have to do it in front of six other people. Six other people found the guts to ski down this horribly icy slope. Six people fell many times, made asses of themselves, got the hats, gloves, skis knocked off of them. But the six picked themselves up, brushed off the snow, and continued down the slope. Even Cindy was scared: Cindy, the one whose stomach was upset from the night before; Cindy, the cautious skier who never took on more than she could handle. But even Cindy kept skiing downhill. I couldn't lose my courage, and I was glad I stuck it out because the bottom half of the slope turned back into novice runs, and it was smooth skiing from then on. We were all glad we had skied down that slope after we had done it — we were all scared beyond comfort, but we had all made it down in seven solid pieces. Despite the ending, we skied directly over to the chair lifts and took another ride up, this time onto an easier slope.

It was there that Rafe and I started.

2

You've got to forget about him, Mitzi. You've got to wipe that picture of his frozen mustache out of your mind ... his face full of melting snow, his ski pants that you told him were ten years out of style. You've got to stop gloating over all the memories, the images that snap back into your mind while you're sitting at your desk, driving through yellow lights, or kissing John. You've got to stop daydreaming about him because the daydreaming can go on and on, even when there's no Rafe around to make it real. You've got to stay away from him even if he wants you.

The lifts were absolutely packed with anxious weekend skiers. They were all dressed up in bold yellows, Kelly greens, Ford Torino oranges. Heads were the status symbol. If you had Head skis and Head outfits on, you were in. Nordicas were popular, Calais, Rossignol, Atomic, Salomon — lots of foreign names tagged on, printed on sides and tips of ankle boots, high boots, insulated black or yellow or orange ski gloves, flowered insulated ski pants that zipped all the way up and down from the ankle to the waist, goggles which snapped on top of knit hats with firm elastic bands ... ski bunnies with expensive outfits, some who could ski and some who just après-skied all day at the lodges. The colors were brazen next to the white snow. Somehow skiers were a group out for fun, snow and that feeling of accomplishment at the end of a long day of downhill.

Everyone had a tan from last weekend's skiing, making us all look like healthy American specimens, with some Europeans and Asians thrown into the mix. Some skiers had "SUN VALLEY" blatantly printed on the backs of their jackets, status symbols of course, but here it meant something. Everyone had patches sewn on to their backsides, ankles, elbows, chests, breasts, gloves. One girl had "DO" on one glove; the other read "DIE."

The day before, Little Spruce had become unbearably hot, but come Saturday, the weather had turned wintery again. I had left my scarf and extra layer of flannel underwear back at the lodge. Now I was freezing.

In Vermont, you went from summer to winter in 14 hours. The chairlift up was chilly, with blizzards at the top, and a raw tough wind that bit at your neck and wrists. Anything exposed was hurting from the gusty winds and snow, and I was suffering. Rafe and I wrapped ourselves in woolen cloaks they passed out before the chair lift zoomed around the bend and swept us up from our behinds. The cloaks didn't stop the biting winds. He covered his face with it so when he talked his voice was muffled. The chair lifts were small and we sat close enough that we could hear each other talk without straining. As we approached the top, I looked down behind myself at the slope, and I started getting frightened again. Thoughts of all those chair lift accidents I had read about winter after winter entered my head, and I suddenly drew the cloak up from behind me to cover my face. I'd peak out from time to time to see if we were near the top, since unloading had to be done instantly. If not, the lift would stop suddenly and that created danger to everyone already on the lifts. At the top of the lift was a big sign that read:

IF YOU DOUBT YOUR ABILITY
TO SKI DOWN THIS SLOPE,
KINDLY INFORM THE CHAIR-LIFT
PERSONNEL AND THEY WILL
GLADLY OFFER YOU A FREE RIDE
BACK DOWN ON THE LIFT.

That was consoling, only I didn't see anyone else jumping back on for the ride down, and I wasn't going to be the first. It wasn't that I doubted my ability; after that last slope off the gondola yesterday, I could ski anything, I thought. The chair lift frightened me, and I knew that once I got back skiing on the slopes, I'd be all right. The cold weather didn't help stop the shaking.

Kathy, Cindy, and Kenny joined us at the top and we all skied together for a while, and stopped from time to time on the sides of the slopes to catch our breaths. Igor and John, the big cross-eyed German, were there too. Kathy asked Igor to rub the Vaseline on my face because my cheeks were icy and she thought she saw frostbite. I couldn't feel anything, so Igor rubbed some on; and even though it was greasy and messy, I was glad he did.

The slope turned terrific; by 11 o'clock, it was packed and skiing was a breeze compared to our early-morning run. We picked the novice and intermediate slopes and it was on them that we skied our best. If one of us fell, all of us would stop and wait until he or she picked herself up and continued on. We all had turns falling, but no one had injuries. Each time, we'd break out laughing, half from relief, half from amusement at watching one another do twists and turns before we'd be off our feet and clumped into the snow. Rafe always managed to wash his face in the snow when he fell. I'd be skiing down in back of him, negotiating a curve, then glancing back up the slope for a moment to see where everyone was. Then, in front of me several yards away, was Rafe standing there, brushing himself off, with a red face and icy mustache. I noticed that he always lost his hat when he fell.

Out of the group, he and I were of the same skiing ability, even though he mentioned later that he had only been skiing for three years. I had skied on and off for a few years myself, but I wasn't far ahead of him in ability. We watched out for each other and seemed to fall the same number of times. I always broke out in giggles and laughter seconds after my falls. I told him I was relieved I wasn't hurt; and when I was laying there on the snow, feeling no pain, I'd start laughing again at how exhilarating it felt to be swept off my feet, sliding and trying to gain control before the final plop into the snow. I told the others not to tell me how much I'd improved since the Sugarbush trip – every time they'd stop and marvel at my progress, I'd lose balance and fall. So they started saying what a lousy skier I was. We all laughed. It was fun to be away from work, bosses, boyfriends, family, and the daily humdrum routines that we all had. It was a heady feeling to be sharing slopes and bunkers with relative strangers, experiencing such an aggressive sport, sharing the falls, the mountains, the views, the snow, the coldness, the wet, raw wind, the pain from heavy inflexible ski boots, the occasional bruise or skin brushes we all had from our falls. We were like a family, but sharing only the good times.

There weren't any bad times in sight.

3

It wasn't that he was so unique. He wasn't a movie star or a late-night talk show host with a super-plus personality. No, he was even too old for me. It was being away, it was the whiskey and waters ... the cold mountain air, the vacation atmosphere that can make any two people fall for each other. It was the laughs on the ski lifts when I'd get cold and he'd tell me to stick my head under the cloak. It was the gluhwein we'd drink at lunchtime when we'd try to talk ourselves off of our lackadaisical behinds and get out there onto the cold slopes and ski again. It was his telling me that it was fat cells that I apparently accumulated when I was a baby that were crying out to FEED ME when I'd get hungry. It was his teaching me how to ski over moguls instead of skiing between them. It was his falling after he'd hit a mogul and me skiing down over them perfectly and twisting into a turn at the end. It was his crying "No fair! I'm the one who taught you, and now you can do it and I can't." It was me falling right after he told me how well I was doing. It was me speeding down and coming to a complete halt at his feet, making a perfect stem christie, stopping on a snowflake, and blurting out, "That felt good!"

Saturday night, we all stayed in at the lodge and had a fondue party. Everyone brought their own booze, and we had a private room at the lodge just for the club. Montana Monica, the skinny and fit anthropologist, brought taped music, and we all painted Bill's cast which was still damp from being put on that morning. I painted his toenails with magic marker pens of different colors, and Rafe roughly painted a knee cap with "Doc" printed under it in gray.

We were all exhausted, what with the long Thursday night bus ride, little sleep two nights in a row, dancing till midnight at the Baggy Knees. I wasn't very sociable by then, but Rafe asked me to dance and I did enjoy dancing with him. He also asked Cindy, Kathy, Terry and Linda. I had my eye out for him now. He had his brown corduroy pants on that didn't meet his ankles, and I considered how much younger and swinging he looked in them instead of in his ten-year-old black stretch ski pants. All of a sudden, he was good looking and not the 40 something year-old man I noticed on Thursday night's bus.

But I avoided him and didn't really care. (So I professed.) Linda was the dancer and she was up there the whole night with whomever would dance with her, slithering to the beats. Kathy, Cindy, and I snuck down to Bill's room ... Bill with the red face from too much drinking and probably high blood pressure, fat Bill who was always jolly but was too old to be attractive, Bill who whiled away young people's time with too much drinking and nibbling at any available food. We knocked on his door and he let us in with a big welcome. He asked us if we wanted to try out his bed with the magic vibrator, all this with much cheeriness, but much underneath sadness because he knew, just as we did, that nobody young and thin and vital considered old fat Bill a sex object. And that's what he was crying out for. He was lonely and Kathy and Cindy were good angels to realize that, and they wanted to make him feel better. So here we were in his room with the vibrating bed. We all took turns vibrating.

We got back to the fondue room and I saw Rafe dancing again, this time with Montana Monica, who always wore a gorgeous ski outfit. The expert skier who led the guys down the super expert NOSE DIVE slope that morning, not falling once. I talked a little with just about everyone, only not the ones who were withdrawn and sat around the tables staring onto the dance floor while they drank. I talked a long time with Bill with the cast on his leg. He still had an accent, and was very undiscouraged and good-natured about his injury. He had been skiing about 12 years and it was his first injury so he "wasn't complaining." We talked about Germany and also about France where I had lived for a few years, and Europe in general; we talked about the German Club in the city that he belonged to and about Volkswagens and Porsches and Citroens. Kathy drew me aside while I was talking to him, and whispered to get up there with Rafe and stick with him. I mimed a *no* and she whispered gently, "You're avoiding it, Becca."

She knew all along why I was talking with Bill. She

wanted me to be with Rafe only I didn't want to be with Rafe. I didn't want to get too close and follow him around and play the typical roles that I always set up between me and guys. Kathy sensed that I was avoiding my particular heartthrobs because in the end I always thought I'd be rejected. I was avoiding pain.

So I watched Rafe dance away with the others and I also noticed before I left for the night that he was sticking with Cindy an awful lot. I just left him alone. He had to see my indifference; he had to sense the fact that, despite the fun we had today together on the slopes, I was letting him go, expressing no interest and not caring to be with him.

Perhaps it was the environment ... the romance of dancing, the idea that if he knew I cared, then he could dump me easily and let me hang on and go dancing with expert hot dog Montana Monica. Or anyone he wanted. He didn't know what a prisoner I could become with a guy, how I would follow them around, how my inner child would come out and I would act moonstruck and aloof. It was the discomfort I was avoiding of not being free and being myself.

I couldn't get close. I couldn't get romantic because I'd lose myself. I didn't know who he was either, or whether he would care for me. How could I let him see that childishness without letting him use it if he wanted? I didn't want the struggle. It was easier to walk away from it.

Cindy, Kathy, and I left the party. Back in the room

that we shared, they told me that Rafe was married. I did a double take and yelled, "MARRIED?!"

"Yeah, didn't you know that?" they both yelled at me.

How could I know that? He never mentioned a wife, children, marriage. That should have been my clue. Apparently, Cindy and Kathy had brought the subject up in conversation at the fondue party, and he told them. Quite simply. I never asked him because it really didn't matter. I found him attractive, a good skiing partner, interesting conversationalist, a doctor which helped make him more attractive, but deep down, it didn't matter.

Rafe wasn't a thing with me yet. Or so I thought.

I feigned emotional trauma, like an infant crying, loud and boisterous, and they laughed at my act. "Oh no, Rafe's' married!" I screamed in deep-down heartache. They knew I cared, but I didn't care that deeply. *Oh well,* I thought, *I'm glad now because there's no threat of my getting serious. He's married and I have the perfect reason for not getting hung up on him.*

Cindy was vibrating on her bed after Kathy put the quarter into the machine that looked like a metronome. Cindy objected because she had drunk too much and her stomach was upset again. She giggled the whole time but got up now and then, went into the bathroom, and came back out looking pale and drawn. She kept complaining about her stomach, and Kathy and I laughed, "You are sick from all the wine and booze at the party."

It was my turn to sleep on the cot; they had the double beds. I objected, but we had said we'd rotate.

Sunday was the day of all days. The slopes were perfect with very few icy patches. The snow from the day before was all packed down from the long day of skiing. There wasn't a cloud in the sky, and our bus took off for Madonna Mountain on the other side of Little and Big Spruce Mountains. We did some cross country skiing, took the lift to the top of Big Spruce, and skied over the top of Madonna where the slopes were more varied. Then we skied downhill, then some uphill trenching which wasn't too pleasant and very exhausting. Finally, we got lift tickets at the top of Madonna Mountain and had them stapled on by the ticket boy.

Little did I realize how easy it was to fall in love since I had never done it before.

We came in at lunch time. Cindy, Rafe, and I limped to the table and chairs because of the pain in our feet. Rafe was affable but talked more to Cindy than me. Cindy got some gluhwein and sipped it too fast. Before long, she bowed her head over the table and slept. Rafe had no choice but to talk to me; and after a while, he knew he had an attentive partner. I got up to get some gluhwein, came back, and offered to share it with him, but he declined. I slurped it down, and before long, my innards were nice and warm, and my cheeks were glowing. We then decided to hit the slopes for the afternoon, and left Cindy there, her head still on the table. We figured she'd be in no condition to ski anyway.

Back on the lift, we talked and talked and hid our heads under our woolen cloaks that still didn't keep us warm enough. He told me about the doctors he worked with at the orthopedic hospital who were nervously facing increased malpractice insurance costs. I told him that doctors should take business courses in med school. We concluded that plumbing is where it's at. He told me about homemade wine and how tasty it is compared to commercial wine. He told me he compares prices on consumer products and does yearly comparisons on price increases vs. size increases, noting how often the consumer pays more per ounce for economy-sized products. I learned how well-read and informed he was. He learned how I could talk a little bit on just about any topic.

He once gestured to put his arm around me, and I stayed cool, not flinching, not welcoming, not turning away. He declined, but I could tell he wanted to touch me. It was a nice feeling to sit there on the lift. By then, the sun was shining and our cloaks were off. It was also nice to know that an interesting guy took a liking to me and wanted to draw near and to look out for each other, ski together, fall together, help each other up and ask, "Are you all right?"

We skied down several times, but by 4 o'clock, we were dragging and falling more frequently, so we decided to quit for the day. We found the group waiting for the bus and parted.

The bus started back home to north New Jersey Sunday evening at 5 p.m. with 36 exhausted but exuberant skiers and three big boxes of picnic lunches provided by the lodge, cases of six packs up on the shelves above our heads, and boxes of pretzels and chips for the six-hour trip. Most of this time, Rafe and I spent sprawled out over two seats, talking and laughing, and his giving me one big, gigantic kiss at the start. I woke up from it in a daze, but conscious enough to notice six other pairs of eyes staring at us. I thought I didn't care. I remembered being proud that such a guy wanted to kiss ME. It had been a long time since a kiss had any impact on me, and it tasted delicious. Sometimes I'd kiss my boyfriend, John, and it would turn into something more intricate in the long run, but I would have easily traded any of his kisses in for that big, fat, juicy one Rafe gave me on the bus.

He held me for a few seconds and drew me right up to him before his lips touched mine, and I remembered thinking afterwards that it was neither too much nor too little, neither too long nor too short. He held his hand on my back and wouldn't let me go, even though at one point of semi-consciousness, I thought we'd better stop. But he kept on, his lips soft, his whole approach soft and ever-so-sweet. It wasn't a sexy kiss at all. It was a warm, *I like you* kiss, but it held much promise of things to come.

After we finished and everyone stopped staring and went back to their seats, I turned to him, flushing, and said, "How come it's easy to get a crush on someone on ski trips?"

To which he replied, "You're easy to like."

From the picnic boxes, there were dried up turkey sandwiches on white bread, and both he and I ate just the meat, throwing the white bread back into the little bags. He said he hated white bread, and I didn't say it, but I hated it too. I had had about five cups of coffee which made it impossible for me to sleep, but later I was glad because it gave me more time to be conscious with him. After three hours on the bus, it got dark, and I wanted to get a blanket, but he walked down the aisle to the back of the bus to get one for me. We spread it over us, and we huddled together automatically, both of us knowing somehow that's what the other wanted to do. We kissed again and again; later on, he started petting my hands and arms *oh so gently*. He rubbed my tummy too, and at one point, even against my very own will, I told him, "Let's cool it."

He jerked himself back into his seat, and we got into an awkward conversation about who calls the shots and who doesn't and who does what to whom, and who is more aggressive, the male or female. He asked why it's up to the woman to say when, and I answered that's only because we've been taught that males are the aggressors and women aren't. I told him a story about a gal who was at a bar talking to a guy on her left, while the guy on her right stroked her leg. The guy on her left asked her if she knew the guy, and she told him she had just met him. He asked her if she wanted the guy to stroke her leg, and she said, no, she didn't, but she was afraid to tell him because she didn't want to hurt his feelings! Rafe snickered, but didn't say anything.

I realized his eyes were brown, the color of chocolate, not blue like my own. He said blue was his favorite color. He turned to face me so I could see his brown eyes better. They didn't mean anything to me then, and I thought later how when feelings turn, one grabs onto everything, every word that was said, everything that was done together. Little hints of affection and warmth that ooze between two people get magnified a thousand times over.

I was giving him a back rub while he rested his head against the seat in front of him. I was sitting back so it was almost effortless to knead my hands around his shoulders and ribs and neck. The look that I saw on the side of his face was one of ecstasy. I knew the feeling. Backrubs, especially after a long weekend of skiing, were sometimes more pleasurable than orgasms. I squeezed hard on every arm muscle down to his elbows and I kneaded just about every muscle he had on his back above his waist. I gave him the fingernail scratch, up and down, down and up, circles, triangles, figure eights. I dug in hard because he had two layers of sweaters and shirts on. Before I started, he had told me that I couldn't hurt him. Now I knew it to be true.

He had a nice back — lean, skinny, ribby. His muscles were taut and stretched thin, unlike my two brothers to whom I gave backrubs when we were all still living at home. Their frames were husky and broad, lined with young strong muscles. His muscles were lean, I liked them lean too.

The bus traveled on, fast, shaky, around the turnpike clover leafs, and I rubbed on. He hadn't moved the whole time. *Was he hoping I wouldn't stop?* My hands got tired and I gave him two or three soft pats, my way of letting him know his backrub was over. Gradually, he took his head off the seat in front, leaned back to where I was, and said, "You're hired."

We changed seats once in a while. At one point, I was getting cramped so I leaned towards the aisle side of my seat. He told me to lean my head on his shoulder and not to worry about him not having enough space to move. I was pleased that he wanted to be near me. I put my head on his shoulder; and even though my body was tired, the five cups of coffee at dinnertime were keeping my brain alive. It was a weird experience to have a tired body but an alert brain. I found him interesting to talk to, so warm and sexy. The eight hours on the bus seemed like one. I was in heaven, and hell was no where in sight.

6

I didn't think I was nervous before the party, but my voice was awfully high-pitched, yelling over to Ed and Mo and Ron in the driveway, much too animated with Elaine, the hostess, as I handed her the half-gallon bottle of Mountain Red. I should have suspected it in my car on the way up, one hour, 35 miles north, and three cigarettes later, unusual for a social smoker who didn't like to drive. For some reason, I pondered this while driving on the highway.

I didn't expect the night to turn out well at all. I had already gone to too much trouble – the long drive, two hours on clothes, make-up and hair-do before. John was still in the hospital, an unexpected twist for the weekend. I wanted him to go with me, because I hated to be unescorted to a party and walk in alone. But the doctors pulled an about face and at the last minute, they wouldn't release him. Something about the anti-coagulants being too strong, and they wanted more tests next week before he left their care.

Mo, a blue-eyed, 5'4" blond with an infectious laugh, was my best friend, and worked in the same building as I. She had heard about Rafe incessantly but had not met him yet. Even though she lived in Collingswood, she and I drove to the party separately since there was a five-mile distance between my mother's house in Walnut Hill and hers. Mo had broken her leg on the ice on the back steps of her townhouse after she got back from another recent ski weekend, and the leg was in a cast. I told her to tell everyone she broke it on the slopes, a much more adventurous story.

I knew Rafe would be there with his wife this time. *The eye opener*, I told myself. My first disappointment. My reason for not getting involved. Seeing her would straighten out my head, stop my fantasies, let me go on with my life the way it should.

He was the first one I saw at the bottom of the basement steps inside. I walked by him, almost briskly, directly to the bar, anxious to get the first glass of wine down quick. He followed me over, and asked if I had come alone.

"Where's your boyfriend?" he laughed. "I saw you walk in with Ed and your girlfriend."

"He's still in the hospital," I lamented, not yet feeling the wine that I had just poured into my slowly warming veins.

"Is that your wife over there?" I pointed to the sandy-haired gal who had been talking to him at the bottom of the steps.

"No, funny thing," he laughed. "My wife's in bed with the flu."

We both looked at each other dead straight in the eyes, then laughed out loud. Try as we might, we couldn't get away from each other, not even for our own good.

By the time I downed two glasses of the red, I was able to talk to him. He was just as breezy and good-humored as ever, always having a good time, always conversational and mellow. He followed me around, sometimes I'd lose him, but he'd always find me. We watched the ski movies together that Ron had brought to the party.

That's when I told him he'd better be careful.

"Why?" he asked quizzically, looking at me straight on.

"Because you're married. You've got a wife and kids to think about. She knows these people, and they know you're hitched. I don't have to worry about that, but you do."

He brushed it aside and said, "They'll always be rumors. You talked up on the slopes about whether we all decide to do something or don't. Let them talk."

"Yeah, you're right," I said, worried.

Ron, the club busybody, had a feint resemblance to Ichabod Crane, skinny, gangly, with a long crooked nose and big ears sticking out. He kept glancing back at the two of us. I told him several weeks ago about Rafe, told him that Rafe was a distraction to me even though he was a married man. "I don't go out with married men," I repeated to him a few times, as though I was trying to convince myself. Ron agreed that I was smart to make my own rules.

So every time Ron turned around, I felt guilty. There's Rafe feeling my ankle and telling me he likes them. There's me leaning on Rafe's back after my fifth glass of wine, and the second ski flick. There's

Ron darting back a glance. There's Mo talking to Ron, occasionally peering over her shoulder and giving me one of her *looks like you're having a good time* grins. Of course she knew I was. The whole week before that, she'd heard Rafe's name a hundred times. She knew me so well that she could have told me exactly what we were talking about.

He seemed interested in everything I said, all that I was, my job, my house-sitting side job that I did for extra cash since I was living back in Walnut Hill with my mother during that time, my tennis and volleyball, my bike riding, even my ancestry. He talked about his kids, finally, and I talked about how it feels to be single in a couple's world. We were at different angles in life, and I found the dissimilarities intriguing. We talked about everything, and let the elephant in the middle of the room sleep.

7

He told me I was too much for him and that he was pleased to be with someone like me. I looked at him in total amazement that anyone could think I was that great. All the men in my life whom I held up on pedestals were men I couldn't get near. And now there was he.

He asked me if I was going straight home after the party, and I told him I was going to Ron's for breakfast. He suggested that we meet beforehand.

"Any ideas?" he asked, looking at me with a big Cheshire grin on his face.

"Well, how about coffee someplace? A diner maybe."

He looked relieved that I didn't suggest something heavier than that, and I was relieved that he was relieved. We both weren't ready. But the pyramid was being built.

"Okay," he said. "Where?"

"I'll see you afterwards," I said, and smiled at him with the toothiest grin I could muster. Somehow, it felt good to look into his friendly brown eyes.

We parted again, and I walked over to Ron who scolded me for not watching more flicks. Some of them were ones he brought, and he wanted to know what I thought about them. I was flying pretty high at that point. Mo was being a good friend by talking to Ron and keeping him distracted. Someone said dinner was on, and quickly Mo and I grabbed a place in line. Rafe was somewhere near the table nibbling on carrot sticks and celery, and both she and I noticed. "That's why he's pencil thin and we're not," I whispered.

As Mo and I dined on stuffed green pepper, Swedish meatballs, and potatoes au gratin, Rafe came over and sat beside me. We talked about calories and why I had weight problems and he didn't. "I eat like a horse," he said as he nibbled on his carrot stick. The smell of meatloaf and homemade bread permeated the party.

"Yeah, sure you do," I practically smirked, taking a huge bite of a fresh Italian roll.

"I do," he insisted. "But I don't gain weight. The guys in college used to kid me about it. One summer, we all ate donuts and coffee for breakfast every morning. We had about four donuts apiece. At the end of the summer, they had all gained ten pounds, and I gained four. It must be my metabolism," he concluded and took another slow sip of his drink.

I finished my meal and noticed that the movies were still going on. I sat beside Stan, the moderator. Stan had retaught me how to ski at Sugarbush that January after I had fallen down so often that I threatened to quit, and I was still grateful to him. He talked my ears off, so I'd have to find a way to get away from him eventually. I pictured Stan as someone who lived alone, an old-fashioned type who was smart, active, always smiling, never obnoxious. *Why can't I fall in love with him,* I lamented. On the ski lift at Glen Ellen, he told me he made a choice between golf and skiing one year, because doing both of them was too expensive. He choose skiing, an easy choice, he claimed, because there was definitely more excitement to it. I had thought Stan was a wealthy businessman, but after he told me the story, I doubted it.

I talked to him awhile, in between his moderating the flick, and pretty soon Rafe walked over to me, and took my hands in his. He smiled full force, standing right in front of me. Then he knelt down, put his hands on my knees, and asked me to meet him out in the backyard.

"Okay," I said. It was an easy decision.

Minutes later, I said good-bye to Stan, and walked up the cellar steps, through the pantry and out the back door into the yard. I had watched Rafe disappear out the Bilko door on the other side of the house and up the steps. We both met back by the trees and stood beside a 20-foot boat parked on the back lawn.

We hugged each other right away, something I had been wanting to do since the bus ride in March. He gave me another one of his million dollar kisses, and from that moment on, I was not the same Becca as before.

"You had to kiss me like that," I whispered into his ear. "You know that's very dangerous."

"You make it hard to be good," he responded, and pulled me apart from himself to look into my eyes. I couldn't believe we were finally together. I smiled at him again, and he drew my lips to his for another dazzling kiss.

He was knocking me out, for I grew dizzier and dizzier. I remember being confused, wondering whether it was the wine, the cool weather that was making me shiver, or Rafe. *It must be Rafe*, I thought, for I had kissed many guys in my lifetime, some even standing in cold weather and drinking a lot of wine. This kiss was beyond all kisses.

He was boney to hug, much less body to wrap my arms around than John. John was big, probably 175 pounds, and tall. But not so tall as Rafe. Rafe couldn't have weighed more than 160. He ran his hands up and down my back several times, sometimes drawing me near, sometimes pulling me away. He took my arms in his hands and stared at me intensely. I stared back, laughing suddenly at how wonderful it was to be at this party, in this backyard with the only man in the world who existed at that moment. John's image grew dimmer and dimmer. He was only 30 miles away in a hospital, but he was 100 miles away from my body and soul. I was beginning to forget what his face looked like—

Someone switched the flood lights on and Rafe and I bolted out of our embrace. Rafe was facing the house and had his eyes stationed on the back cellar door. "Someone's coming," he whispered, and I turned around to watch some man walking around the back yard. Eventually he saw us, then turned around and went in. The flood lights went out and we were alone again.

We looked at each other, and I asked if he knew who it was. He said he couldn't make him out and wasn't sure if he would have known the fellow anyway. All the clubbers didn't necessarily know each other since some didn't go on ski trips but just maintained membership for the social aspects.

A few seconds or minutes, I don't know which, passed until he took me into his arms and we kissed again and again and again. I was swaying back and forth, partly to maintain my balance while in his arms, and partly from the six glasses of wine. I was shivering from the cold, and I eventually knocked over my glass of wine resting at our feet. Some of it spilled onto my shoe, and I told myself that it wasn't important that my brand new pair of expensive soft-as-butter Italian leather pumps were stained.

After a few minutes more of Rafe's fantastic hugs and kisses, we decided to go back in. We didn't know if it was a good idea to go in together after being away from the party for so long. We tiptoed over to the side of the house, had one more embrace, and said we'd meet after the party for coffee somewhere. He slipped in the front door, and I found a flight of steps which led down to the basement. When I got downstairs, the party was still going strong, and everybody was doing their own thing, so I wasn't too worried about whether they noticed we were both missing for a while. Elaine was setting up desserts and coffee at separate tables and I offered to help. Afterwards, I quickly found my way over to the desserts table, and helped myself to homemade shoe-fly pie, and a couple of brownies. Then I joined the coffee line and out of the corner of my eye, I saw Rafe talking to someone at the bar. He shot me a quick glance which penetrated me like a laser beam.

He was disinterested in desserts, and I was amazed at how a guy could ignore such appetizing dishes. It was past midnight by now, and Mo was helping herself to a big plateful too. The two of us sat down with plates bulging.

Later on, the dancing started, and Rafe and I did a few slow ones out on the floor. It was neat that everyone was doing their own thing, and I decided that he and I had nothing to worry about. Except for Ron's too long stares every now and then, I was comfortable and having the best time of my life. Ron came over and asked me to dance a few times, never saying anything about Rafe and me, but somehow, I knew that he knew. He was the only one I had to worry about. Mo could keep things to herself, all the things she knew about Rafe and me, but Ron had been a long-standing member of the club and knew personally just about everyone. He could start and end rumors quicker than Hollywood.

It was neat to dance with Rafe. He was a good dancer, not the best I'd ever danced with, but good.

At the end of each dance, he'd squeeze me tight and let me go, and we'd look at each other as if we knew important things were going to happen.

Ron kept asking if I was coming to his house for breakfast, and I kept telling him I probably would. He named the rest of the clubbers who were coming, Mo included, and told me I could stay overnight if I wanted. He had a spare bedroom so there were plenty of beds and he mentioned that Rich and Mark brought their sleeping bags.

I knew it would be a late night, but I also knew that I had a date with Rafe after the party, and I hadn't been able to determine how to swing Ron's breakfast with coffee with Rafe. I kept evading Ron's questions about when I was ready to leave. I got the impression that the whole thing hinged on me.

Mo kept complaining about the pain in her ankle. She and Rafe and I were talking and she mentioned it to him. He told her to sit down while he looked at her cast. I had to laugh at the sight of Mo with her leg stretched out on a chair so he could get a good look, his feeling her toes sticking out, pressing in on her knee to watch if she reacted in pain. She looked at me, almost giggling. I gradually drifted away from them and talked to someone else.

A few minutes later, I helped myself to more wine at the bar. Rafe came up beside me. "Wanna go for a ride?"

I looked at him for a few seconds, thinking of all the things that could happen between us if we were truly alone. I said surprisingly, without hesitation, "Yes."

He took off and I waited a few minutes until he was gone before I slipped up the steps and out the front door. I found him in a Ferrari sportscar with the headlights on. He pulled up to me in the driveway.

We took off for a short drive on the country roads. It was a beautiful night with a clear starlit sky, perfect for a romantic mood. He drove about a mile, the Ferrari breathing heavily and whirring in second gear. I told him it was a neat car, and he said, "Thanks."

He told me he had always kept junkers until two years ago when he bought this one. He pulled over to the side of a long, lonely road and turned the motor off. Then he pulled me to him and gave me a beautiful squeeze, right up next to his body. I was practically sprawled across the front seat. Gradually, out of breath, I drew back and sat up straight in my seat. We laughed because it was the first time, the very first time, that we were able to be completely alone, safely alone, and able to relax. I had on a denim skirt, buttoned from waist to hem, and a white embroidered Oriental blouse that dipped mildly at the neck, with buttons leading to the waist.

I never did get to Ron's breakfast party. I got home late, after a long drive. I also noticed when I got there in the early morning that some of the buttons on both my blouse and skirt were missing. We didn't go all the way but we sure had a good time trying not to get there.

✳ ✳ ✳

It was weeks before Rafe and I could see each other again. It wasn't as much my problem as his. He couldn't be seen in public. He had to get his house renovated before the next winter months. Everyone knew him in the sports car he drove. His orthopedic practice kept him busy six days a week. Plus, he was married. He described himself as a family man, and didn't want to make any breaks. Why did he think of himself as a family man when we were out hugging and kissing in his car? I asked him this, and he said this was the first time he had put himself in this kind of situation.

Of course, I interpreted that in many ways. It could mean I was his first affair. Or his first ski club affair. Or the first time that these circumstances arose. I asked him what he meant by "You are my first." He mentioned the ski club, whatever the hell that meant. It didn't matter to me whether or not I was his first affair, although it would have been a big boost if I were that irresistible. That even a family man couldn't leave me alone. Like marrying a virgin – being the first one. I would have liked to be his first, but I didn't want to hear it unless it were true. I wanted his honesty.

Rafe was attractive, at least I thought so, and it wasn't inconceivable to me that other women would fall for him. I also didn't want him fooling around with my emotions, because my emotions could make me either sink or swim.

We finally got together on my mother's front porch. It was May now, a long time for two hot people to be away from each other. He would call me at work about twice a week, unexpectedly, and it always made me tingle. My Mom was down the Jersey shore that week. Finally, on that Tuesday night, he told his wife that he had a hospital meeting up in Newark. He headed over to my mother's house after work.

I was awfully nervous about it, meeting him there, the place where I grew up. It was a sacred place, much too sacred to make love to this stranger in spite of my feelings for him. Nobody did illicit things like that in this home, and besides, whose bed would we use? My father's, whose hadn't been slept in in years since his death? My own that I had slept in, night after night, with the dog at the foot? On the third floor where it was dusty and spooky, where my mother put roomers when the university opened in the fall? How about the guest room with the four poster bed, legs stretching up so tall that guests had to practically jump on it to keep their balance?

I had picked the front porch, and all the worrying I did about that wasn't necessary. Nothing happened. At least nothing big, tempestuous, or illegal. We had a good time – a good time for me was just being with Rafe. But that was all. He looked great as usual, and a little nervous himself. He had brought a bottle of white German wine with him, and I had a bottle on hand also. We opened my bottle of chilled Charles Krug Chablis. He drank the first glass down in a hurry, but I declined since I had had a drink at dinner before he came, an unusual practice for me to drink alone. He kept insisting that I join him, but I told him I wanted to enjoy him naturally, without the benefit of booze. He was let down, I could tell, but he drank on. After a few minutes, he started to relax and didn't seem like he was in such a hurry.

It was my idea to sit on the porch. It was nice and breezy, but he headed towards the living room. He said the house didn't look so bad. He had mentioned that because I told him what a disinterested housekeeper my mother was, although she always kept her living room cleared of all the junk when we were kids. But we were the ones who had to keep it well-dusted and vacuumed for her guests. The rest of the house, other than the living room, the hallway, and the third floor bedrooms, for which she'd get money renting them out, were quite unkempt. I was always embarrassed about it and rarely invited people in. But here he was, an important person in my life right now, in this three-story Walnut Hill stone home, a mess inside.

He walked over to my mother's silver spoon collection, some of which were antiques, and commented on them. We then sat in the living room for a while, he drinking wine and me giggling a lot. I was happy. My new Schwinn 10-speed bicycle was parked in the middle of it, and he commented on how shiny it was. I told him it was getting rusty because my bike partner wasn't around.

"Is he the one who was in the hospital?"

"Yes," I responded.

"He's not around anymore?"

I nodded affirmatively with my head.

"You mean he died?"

"No, silly," I said. "I just don't go with him anymore."

We couldn't hold back the laughter. I almost wanted to call John and tell him that this new guy thought he was dead. John would appreciate the humor.

Rafe was winding down gradually, and soon he grabbed me, put his arms around my waist and gave me a gorgeous welcome kiss.

"How ya doin', kid?" he asked.

"Fine, kiddo," I responded.

"You're lookin' good," he said, looking directly into my eyes for the first time that night. I could tell he was almost totally blitzed.

8

"Do you want to move out to the porch?" I asked. "It's too dusty in here."

Rafe was sneezing already. He went out to his sports car, got an allergy pill, and drank it down with the wine.

"You know," he said, "this isn't such a bad house. To think you were here all the time growing up while I was in the next neighborhood down. I remember when the high school you went to was a big open dirt field. We played baseball there and fished in the stream." He was talking about the section of the town where I lived. He lived in Moorestown. "I remember when the high school was being built," I said. "My father took us over to see it. I was in grade school then and he told us that's where we'd be going to school in a few years."

He was surprised that I remembered the dirt field. "I thought you'd be too young to remember that."

Rafe was only eight years older than me, but he always talked about the "old days" and "way back when" as if he were an old man. I accused him of being 80.

"Well, don't forget, kid. There were milk trucks and gas lanterns on the streets of North Jersey when I was a kid."

"Well, don't forget, kid," I mocked him. "I remember them too. I was a little girl, before grade school even, when my mother had a milkman, a bread man who came in twice a week with fresh bakery stuff, and a butter and egg man. The latter's name was Mr. Patterson, and in those days, those men were like friends to my mother. She knew all about their families, their wives, their children, where they lived. She even knew what religion they were, whether or not they went to church, which church, and if he was the same religion, there was even a closer bond."

"Was she in love with any of them?" he asked.

I was almost shocked at the question. My mother in love with another man?

"I don't think so," I said rather guardedly. It never occurred to me that that could be true. "They were friends," I continued. "They were like family. She trusted them, and I'm sure she told them things she'd never tell us. Or my father. They were each other's therapists. She knew the butter and egg man for years. My father and mother would drive up to his farm in the country with us a few times to get chickens and make a Sunday visit. He'd deliver his eggs once or twice a week, stay for about 20 minutes, sitting in the kitchen writing out her order on a plain slip of paper with a pencil he kept behind his ears. He always joked with us; and once in a while, he'd grab us and we'd have to give him a hug. She liked Mr. Patterson. He was much older than she, but I think he was like her father, kindly, odd, a simple person with a simple job. I am sure he is dead by now. When he gave up his business, I know she missed him."

I stopped, then looked at Rafe. I had talked enough. Rafe was still listening though so I took it up again.

"Eventually her milkman, breadman, and butter and egg man were replaced by supermarkets. Even her grocer, Mr. Sarner, around the corner, went out of business. He had the freshest fish on Fridays for Catholics. Then the Catholics were allowed to eat meat on Fridays and he lost the fish market too."

He was staring out the front window, unresponsive.

9

I asked him again if he wanted to sit on the porch. He looked at me sheepishly, and I got the impression he was afraid he'd be seen.

"Don't worry," I assured him. "No one can see us out there." My mother's next-door-neighbor was the only one who could possibly see us on the porch; but it was ten o'clock, and I could see her TV still on through her bay window on the side of her house.

"What's her name," he asked, trying to seem off-handed.

"Miss Dresher. Her brother's an optometrist in town."

"Okay, I don't know her." He grabbed my hand and led me out to the darkened porch, two wine glasses in hand, and the bottle of wine.

In between all my talking, he put his arms around me and nuzzled. I coaxed him into face rubs. After the first ten minutes, he started relaxing and stopped watching all the passers-by and cars.

We tickled each other a little on the big iron glider that my mother had painted red. I was having fun. It was like being a kid again. I looked at him and started laughing.

"What?" he asked, grinning back.

I couldn't talk.

"Have more wine with me, please," he begged. "It's really good." He sat up and started pouring me some.

"No," I insisted. "I really don't want anymore."

"Okay." He seemed resigned now. "You're a better woman than I am."

We both giggled and I went on with the face rub. His skin was very smooth for a guy. Later on, when I became more familiar with the rest of his body, I discovered that his chest and back were smooth too. *Smoother than mine?*

I confronted him with it one time, and he didn't say anything. I thought he was embarrassed because he wasn't hairy like most men. But his legs were hairy, and I thought he was happy about that.

It was out on the porch, in the cool breeze of the summer night, when I told him I couldn't go to bed with him.

"Why?" He darted up on one elbow and looked at me intensely.

"Well, Rafe," I started, staring straight ahead at the sky and across the street to the Edelmans' rooftop. "I guess I must protect myself. I can't let myself fall for you."

"Why worry about that now?" he insisted. "Why don't we do what you said a while ago. Play it by ear. Let things happen. You had that attitude before."

He was right. I did at the party after the ski trip. Something had changed, whether it was mother's house or my own conscience or Mom's ghost chaperoning us on the porch.

"You're the kind of guy I can fall for."

He drew a deep breath and stared out straight ahead across the street at the Edelmans' house. At one time, four members of the family lived there and it bustled with activity. They moved and now it had been empty for a long time.

"You've got to protect yourself, Rafe. When we go to meetings, I'm going to want to be with you. And people will talk. It'll get back to your wife. Some of the club people know her and know you're married. You'll be found out, and I'm just saying you'd better be careful."

He didn't say anything to that, which scared me. Each time I mentioned "marriage," he turned his head away from me and grimaced. He was silent, and I tried to change the subject.

"What's that got to do with now?" he asked, almost annoyed.

"What I'm saying is that I won't let myself be turned on by you."

His eyes got wide and his face drooped. "Well, why don't we just avoid each other at meetings, just like every other couple splits from each other during parties. Everyone talks to everyone else, and then when it's time to go home, the couples go home together."

"Yes, but we're not married," I implored. I heard myself saying that word quite a few times. Apparently it bothered me a lot. "We don't have the luxury of going home together. I mean," I continued, almost on a mission, "I'm not the possessive type, but I do know how I'd feel if I saw your arm around another skier. If I'm having an affair with you, I have no rights, no possession. I'm not that cool that I can do it."

He seemed resigned. "I don't know, Becca." He drew a deep breath, and took another sip of wine. "If you feel that way, you feel that way. I think some of your attitudes are high schoolish, though."

Those words rang like rusty iron bells in my ears. It meant he didn't understand my position. He had no idea what it was like being single. He also didn't realize what being with him was doing to my once-sterling reputation. I told him so and he was quiet again. That disturbed me.

"I only ask," I said, realizing I was talking as if I were running a United Nations session, "that you understand my position. Perhaps you don't feel this way – apparently you don't. But my reasons are valid, I believe, and I think a lot of women would feel the same."

He was lying down beside me staring at the porch roof. His hand was rubbing his forehead. I had stopped the face rub. We weren't touching each other at all.

"I guess you ought to know," he said, "that I can't continue seeing you at all unless we go to bed." He said it more of a fact than a threat. "I'm frustrated right now. I don't know what to do with you. I want to hold you and kiss you and make love to you. But knowing how you feel, that you don't want to continue on, and knowing what sex means to you, I feel wrong in touching you."

I started getting uncomfortable. The words "high schoolish" were still swarming in my head. It wasn't the first time someone told me that ... that my sexual attitudes were immature, but it was usually said by men trying to get into my pants.

Rafe sat upright again, leaning on his elbow. He stared down at me. I could see the outline of his mustache and forehead in the light of Miss Dresher's porch. I looked up at him, my face was lower than his, and I stroked his forehead. I felt guilty about touching him at all.

He bent down and kissed me, and we started another round of passionate kissing. Only I wouldn't let myself get turned on. I felt like a stiff board, and even his million dollar kisses didn't loosen me up. He got into it, and after a few minutes, he stopped and looked at me pathetically. He had a big question mark on his forehead; the skin between his eyes was all wrinkled and I saw a frown appear for the first time on his face. *Oh God*, I thought. *This is awful.* Suddenly all the fun that he and I were having turned into a problem, turned serious. I didn't want that to happen.

"Don't you feel anything?" he whispered. His brown beautiful eyes searched mine intensely. "Okay then," he said after noting my silence. He drew back and stared at the sky out past the porch roof.

He turned his head around and looked at me. He smiled so nicely. I could tell he wasn't angry or hurt.

He accepted what I said. Again, Rafe let me be the boss. I liked him for that. He was aggressive in his own way, but he wouldn't push. He didn't try to convince me I was wrong. I could tell he wasn't happy about it, but I could count on him not to give me hassles.

We both lay there, and grabbed each other and hugged for a few minutes. There wasn't much to say, so we just opted for the comfort of each other's bodies. I didn't want him to go – I didn't want him to stay.

Goddam but his body was warm.

10

Finally, we got up, walked over to the side of the porch, bent over to look at his watch which lit up by Miss Dresher's porch light, and saw that it was getting late. He asked to use the bathroom, and I told him reluctantly how to get to it upstairs on the second floor. It was a mess up there, too. Afterwards, he came down without comment, and I helped him brush hair off his clothes and straighten his tie. He stood up to my mother's hallway mirror, and as he combed his mop of thick, wavy, black and gray hair, he asked me if he looked like he just came from a hospital meeting.

I laughed and took pains to remove lingering light brown hairs that may have been mine.

He walked through the dining room and into the kitchen to pick his wallet up off of the table. I stood there in the hallway watching him walk back through the dining room. His legs were long and skinny, and I thought to myself how great it was that a guy like him was there with me.

I wondered what he saw in me. Was it just the sex? I knew that was important to him, but I didn't think it was the only thing he was after. What was it about him that I still didn't feel used? I wanted to go to bed with him too, but my body wouldn't let me. It was shutting down. It couldn't overcome the body-mind connection. And my mind objected to his being married.

"Well, I gotta' go, kiddo," he said, turning to me, putting my cheeks in his hands. He bent down and kissed me again, and I felt like I was on the bus to Vermont, only without 15 other people peering down our necks.

He pulled away from me. We were safe, and it felt good.

I patted him on the behind, his small, skinny, hipless behind. It was the kind that disappeared in one's hands.

"If you ever change your mind, you know where to find me. I won't close any doors behind me. Will you remember that?"

By this time, I was tired, and my eyes were half-open, half-closed. I managed to look him in the eye though, and wondered if I could stay away from him like I said I would. I didn't answer him. I couldn't. I watched him walk down the porch steps, down the walk, and down the short steps to the sidewalk. As he got into his car, he turned around and blew me a kiss.

I went upstairs and flung myself on the bed, and of course, I couldn't sleep. It messed up my whole week at work.

It was July, months later, before we were able to get together again. I was house-sitting for some friends who had gone down to Norfolk, Virginia, on a business/pleasure trip. It was a Friday night. Before that, I had called him about one week after we had said goodbye on my mother's porch. I asked him if a woman had a right to change her mind. He laughed into the phone and said, "Of course."

He asked me later what changed my mind. I started to explain, but the words ran into each other and I ended up saying, "Oh I don't know," about five times. I finally gave up, and said, "Rafe, don't ask me."

"Okay," he said. "I won't."

And we went on to another subject.

To be honest, I can't remember much of what happened at the house. But I do know this: my body would not unfreeze. It wouldn't respond as I lay naked on the bed like a plank of wood. Afraid to breathe. Afraid to move. I wanted him so badly, but my body — *or was it my brain?* — said no.

My *New Baltimore Catechism,* written by Father Michael A. McGuire, explains that by the sixth commandment of God, "Thou shalt not commit adultery," we are commanded to be pure and modest in our behavior.

This romance was totally against my religion and upbringing. Dad came home faithfully every night after a hard day's work, had dinner with us, watched some TV, read the paper and went to bed. On Fridays, he'd hand his salary over to my mother, minus the ten dollars he needed for gas.

This is what I was used to. This is how I grew up, with a father home every night and a mother who tended to their kids.

What was different about this with Rafe? Where were his kids? Where was his wife? Why was he with me and not her?

In my mind, once you marry, you stay faithful until you either die or get divorced. A married man has an unfair advantage over an unmarried woman. He has someone to go home to — she doesn't.

I was breaking a commandment, charting untraveled territory in my family, and I thought at the time that I could quite possibly be headed for Hell.

11

Rafe wasn't at the next party, and I missed him. He knew the hosts and I expected him to be there with his wife. *No matter,* I lied to myself. *Better not to complicate things.* I wanted to see her, though. I wondered what kind of woman he had picked out above the rest. I wondered if she was like me. If she was tall and liked sports. Or short and bookish. I was athletic and I wanted her to be athletic too.

I was quiet that night. The party was just okay. Howie, a member of the club, was there along with a few other guys who I knew could fill up my time with talk. It wasn't a bad party, but I was so used to having him there – sneaking out the back door with him someplace. Now I had to be straight, and it wasn't the same.

Howie had no idea about Rafe and me. The only thing I worried about now was how we'd act at the fall parties, when things started heating up for the winter ski season. How was I going to handle Ron, the town gossip, and Rafe since Ron would know? He was very perceptive. And Rafe and I weren't a thing like some other couples at the club who had been having affairs for several years, almost from the beginning. They were well-established and no one asked questions. But Rafe and I were new. Questions would be asked.

I told Mo one time that I felt like a bad person, sneaking around with him, talking to him on the phone during the week. She looked at me and said, "Well, yeah, I guess in a way. But you're having a good time with him, aren't you?"

"Yes, definitely."

"Well, like you said, Becca. Enjoy it for what it is. Don't worry about being bad. Just don't get too involved, or fall for him too much."

Not too involved? I questioned myself a hundred times. *How do I not get too involved?*

"Sometimes I feel like he's using me," I told her another time.

"Well, you're using him too, aren't you?" She was being my devil's advocate.

"In a way, yes," I admitted. "But I don't want it to be like that. I don't want to be just an object, an affair. I'm using him for something, and he me, but there's more than that. I enjoy him so much, and he enjoys me."

"That's all you need," she finalized.

12

In August, I stayed at a friend's house in Collingswood who had gone to Virginia Beach for a few days. I called Rafe and told him the address and asked if he could come over. He said he'd have to do some rearranging and would let me know.

Meanwhile, I was seeing a few other guys. Nothing serious. There was Ron from the club who invited me at the end of summer to the New Jersey shore with his parents. He wasn't the most stimulating company, and he was a little too old for me. But we rode bikes and took some long foot hikes to the next town and window-shopped. We both walked at the same pace, and at one point, I said, "We walk well together."

He agreed. "I walked with the gals from Ocean City and they're always three blocks behind me. Or," he laughed between his teeth, "they don't want to go on walks. I get up early in the morning, and if there's nothing to do, I start walking someplace. Anyplace."

"It clears the head," I mumbled.

That's all we had in common. When he got a few drinks in him, he got loquacious, but for a man his age, he was very unsure of himself. At most he would say, "Yeah," in his deep voice or "Ahuh." That got tiresome after a while, and sometimes I'd just stop talking.

Once in a while, Ron would bring up the ski club, and Rafe's name would pop up. A few times, I suspected he was throwing the name out to check my reaction. He was gossipy. When we were on ski trips to Vermont, when Rafe and I were bundled up under the lift blankets, I'd see Ron watching us out of the corner of his eyes from the chairlift ahead of us.

I never gave him the satisfaction of reacting, and I didn't pursue the subjects that included Rafe. The one thing I didn't want was news of Rafe and me spread around the club. And Ron was good at spreading news. I think he liked to have something on everyone.

There was another fellow from work that I saw occasionally. Alex. Tall, blond, extremely intelligent. A magna cum laude through university. He'd call me about three times a year to go out, never in; and always after we'd spend an evening together, I'd wait for him to call again. Nothing would happen for months. His indifference made me extremely interested in him. He was elusive, aloof, and unsure of himself, but unlike Ron, he was witty and seemed curious and interested. He'd ask me questions about myself and respond to my answers. Sometimes I'd get the impression that he threw the conversational ball at me so he wouldn't have to talk.

He was frustrating though. When he did talk, he wouldn't reveal anything about himself. He'd muse over football, baseball, golf, work, parents, but only in between would he throw in bits and pieces about his unhappy childhood, and on occasion, allude to his present dissatisfaction with himself and his life.

He never gave any indication of how he felt about me. I often thought he secretly disliked me.

Unfortunately, I was extremely and overly impressed with him. He was very tall, like my oldest brother, and uncommunicative, like my father. Sometimes he'd sit in a roomful of people and not say one word. Other times, he'd say something that was unusually brilliant. But I always felt that it was an effort for him to open his mouth. I caught myself thinking that I'd rather he not say anything than feel forced to say something just to be nice. I never confronted him with that point, but I resolved to, as soon as I knew that he wouldn't be embarrassed about it. But then, I finally reasoned, he'd be completely silent about it, as he didn't want to say much.

One time, we were invited to a picnic with the people at work and their families. We were all drinking beer, and I thought this would loosen him up. But the only thing it did was loosen me up. Everyone at the party knew him and liked him so they weren't surprised at his silence. He was in the upper echelons of management at our company and was well-respected. When Kat and Joe invited him over for dinner sometime in the future, Kat added that she thought it might be too far for him to travel.

"Where do you live, Alex?" she asked, turning to him from the kitchen range.

"Valley Hunt, above Hamilton Township."

"Well, is that too far to come to dinner? Joe and I have been meaning to invite you over for the longest time."

"No place is too far for a good meal," he quipped.

That was about the extent of his conversation at the picnic. But as soon as we got into the car on the way home, he started talking about the picnic, the other guests, things that were said, and the people who said them.

"You know," I said to him, commenting about the way he was. "You are funny. You are so quiet around the crowds but so talkative when you're alone with me."

"I never was good with crowds," he admitted. "It's hard to talk to a lot of people at once."

I always had the opposite problem. I was good with crowds and stunk when alone with men. It had a lot to do with my father.

"When you're raised in a big family like I was," I continued, "you're used to being in a crowd. The whole world is a crowd, actually. Another family."

"That's one way to look at it, I s'pose." He always said "I s'pose."

All the way home, he asked me questions. How was the mind control course they offered at work? Did I like the salesman?

"No," I answered, "I thought he was a good leader, but a lousy salesman."

"I'm glad to hear that," he affirmed. "I thought he

was a jerk."

"I agree with you," I said. "I think he was too pushy. I don't like pushy people. And," I continued, "when I said I'd go home and think about signing up, he asked me if I had trouble making decisions."

"You're kidding," he said, turning to me in amazement. "That's the same thing he said to me."

"Well, what'd you get out of the course?" He wanted to know.

"I thought, primarily, it was a good exercise in getting to know a new group of people. A group dynamics type of thing. But I've been through them before and know what they're all about, so that was nothing new. I still learned some stuff, things I didn't know about myself," I continued earnestly, glad to have the opportunity to talk about myself.

"Like what?" he asked.

"Like learning the impressions we can give people. One guy said that if I fixed my hair up and used the right make-up, I could be a very attractive woman!"

He looked at me sheepishly, taking his eyes off the road momentarily. "I don't know if I'd like a course like that," he said. "How did you feel about the criticism?"

"It was good in a way, I guess," I said, looking out into the road and remembering the humiliation of hearing those statements. "I must be getting wise in my old age because criticism used to knock me down to the floor. My new attitude is I care about myself, I know who I am, and I accept myself – completely. If the rest of the world doesn't like it, too bad. I have to like myself, and I come first."

If only those words were true. I was reciting the mantras of the course, still new to me. I had realized early on that my self-esteem was interminably low.

"Of course," I rambled on, with the seeming wisdom of an older person who has come to grips with her life, "I want people to like me and accept me. Very much so. But I'm not hanging on to it anymore. I'm not out to prove what a wonderful person I am. I'm not perfect, never will be. I make mistakes. I make them every day, been making them for years. But I'll be making them 'til I'm dead, and when I stop making them, that means I'm not doing anything, and I might as well be dead."

"Well, geeze," he breathed in and out, trying to take my mission statement all in. "That's amazing. Maybe I should have taken the course. I want to feel that way."

This was something new for me to hear coming from a top officer of the company. "Well, you could feel that way, and you are a worthwhile person. Everyone is. Only everyone doesn't know it. I guess that's called confidence – when you think you're gold no matter what the rest of the world thinks."

"Do you think you're gold?" he asked me, still full of questions.

"Yes, I do now," I answered, unaware of how ridiculous my claim to this kind of confidence was.

"Didn't always. In fact, for most of my life, I thought I was dirt." I could see he wasn't believing that one.

"Honest?" he asked.

"Yup. Very definitely." And that was a true statement.

"Do you think you'll get headstrong and become narcissistic?" he asked again, his questions still coming out profusely.

"I don't think so." I sounded resolute.

"What if someone treated you like copper instead of gold? Would you drop them?"

He could be corny at times.

Then there was Brody. Brody was tall with honey-colored hair, a beautiful body, and a brown, neatly trimmed beard. He looked like the handsome Jesus Christ they depict in pictures. Brody was very athletic, played soccer 40 hours a week while everyone else was working, and worked a few times a week while everyone else was playing soccer or golf or tennis. He was infantile in a lot of ways, still a child who never matured. He was someone I mothered. Every gal has a guy like that at one point in her life. Brody should have been called "Moody." He went through moods where, one day he was all sweetness and light, and the next day, he wouldn't talk to me. He did that with his family, his teachers, and his friends. But mostly, he did it with me.

"Brody, it's not that bad. It's really not," I would coax him during one of his down-and-outs.

"The world stinks," he'd growl, and twist his lips like he was ready to bite me.

"Yes, it does," I'd counter. "But sometimes it doesn't. Ya gotta stay positive."

"Fooey," he'd say. "There's no sense in continuing."

If I hadn't known him for a long time, then I'd have taken his threats more seriously. But I had already identified this phenomenon as mood swings, not suicide talk. So far, I hadn't been wrong.

But Brody equated suicide with just having a lousy day. There were some days when he wouldn't budge out of his melancholy.

I often suspected that studying philosophy in college didn't help pull him out of it. I rationalized that some people who study philosophy are apt to be introspective in some way. Inhibited, introverted, everything inward towards self. Brody wasn't the happy-go-lucky guy who shouted his dissatisfactions to get them off his chest. No, he'd sit in a corner and brood for hours if I so much as looked at him cross-eyed.

"Brody, come on," I argued one night. "Let's get some food." I was hungry, and it had been ages since a guy took me anyplace. I hadn't seen Rafe for weeks, and Alex was doing his usual six-month hiatus. The shore days with Ron were over anyway.

"I'm not hungry," he barked. "Besides I don't want to face the world."

I knew deep down that Brody was waiting for my mother to come home and make dinner. He had a knack for sitting around, brooding, reading the newspaper, then perking up when she'd come home. A short time after dinner, when all the dishes were piled up in the sink and on the counters, Brody would disappear, and I'd find him later, curled up behind a book in the living room, enjoying one of his moods again. He would continue ignoring me.

Of course, this is what I didn't need while waiting for things to happen between Rafe and me. My ego wasn't exactly 100%, and Brody didn't help. He could have been a supporter, but he always gave me a hard time. It was this hard time that I kept coming back for, I guess.

Mo called one day and said that Ron had put his house up for sale and was moving to the Jersey Shore with his aging parents, to help take care of them. He had quit the ski club and sold his skis. "No skiing at the ocean," he said to Mo.

13

It was that time of the year when your bones told you that spring was coming. A big doom of rain, sleet, and snowstorms that incapacitated the region for months had finally passed. The days were growing longer, and each morning the awakening process became more pleasant. No longer did I dress for work in the dark and come home in the dark. Daylight came and woke up all the workers and didn't leave us until we were well on our way home in the evening. It was the promise of soft warm breezes whistling through the air that got us through our days and made our cool nights an anticipation of the next day's warmth.

Rafe and I were squeezed in the front seat of his Ferrari. It was as unique as he was.

We had been there before, in his car, a year before, the night we spent our first minutes alone. How good it felt then to be able to talk and not whisper, to hug and not be ashamed. It was no different now. I couldn't think of another place I'd rather have been than squeezed in the front seat of his car, my knees just about touching my nose, bent up so that the slit at the bottom of my dress was embarrassingly revealing. Rafe wasn't a leg man. I could tell. His eyes never noticed anything I wore below my waist. He wanted everything to do with my blouse, my jumper, my buttons down the front.

Things had been going well with us. There was

only one hint of danger in the air about our becoming friends at the club. His wife was away again for a few days with the kids; and as unfair as I thought that was, that her vacations had to be shared with the kids and his didn't, I was grateful for the setup. It gave us a chance to be together, a rare occasion, even if it was only a necking date in his car, parked in front of the house that separated us from rows and rows of trees, shrubs and bushes. We had driven around our old neighborhoods for a while, him reminiscing about his high school days, pointing out houses where old girlfriends lived. "You're not allowed to pass them while I'm in this car, Rafe," I demanded.

"Don't worry. They're old girlfriends. High school types."

I didn't mind that his car meandered around Moorestown with me. I was just glad to be with him. Period. He talked about high school, the time he parked his car in front of "that house" only to come out moments later with the girl on his arm and watching his car roll down the street, eventually crashing into a lamppost. I didn't even mind his telling me about horseback riding at the very same paddock where my father worked as a horse tenderer up in Hamilton. Rafe rode the horses as a young man. My dad had three kids by the time he worked there, years earlier than Rafe's era. The Depression had started, so Dad, who had no real skills then, grabbed at anything he could find. I got the picture that Rafe was a rich man's son, which made me think, *what the hell is he doing with me?* I certainly wasn't born into the upper edge of the middle class, but he was. It was one thing that I suspected could eventually undermine the relationship.

He kept referring to those days as the "good ole days," and again I accused him of being an old man. "You're only eight years older than me by the way," I chided him for the second time that night.

He showed me a picture of himself in high school. It was a faint resemblance to the person I knew and loved. No features were identifiable between him then and now, except his mouth.

"You're trying to tell me I have a big mouth," he laughed as I pointed that fact out.

"You have a nice mouth, but it's the only feature that's still you." I had noticed the absence of gray hair in the picture but didn't say it.

We did a lot of hugging in the car after a while. It took some time before we warmed up to each other. The moon was peaking through the trees like it had done a year before in the ski club member's wheat fields. That same old friendly moon.

"It's still shining down on us, Rafe," I whispered, and cuddled him closer.

"Somebody's looking out for us, kid," he responded.

I lifted my head up. "And stop calling me kid. You're not that old." I buried my head back into his chest.

14

It wasn't always sweetness and light between us, and danger lurked behind closed doors. There was the ever-present threat of word getting back to his wife that her husband had a girlfriend with whom he spent his skiing weekends. His friends in the club were closely and strongly allied to his wife, and he couldn't count on them to keep closed mouths. Not that Rafe tiptoed around me or our relationship. He was quite open about it. Foolishly so, I thought.

On ski weekends, he didn't hide his affections. He openly pursued me and waited for me in the lobbies while I got dressed in the women's dorm. He'd call me on the telephone to see if it was me who had used up all the hot water before he got his shower. He saved seats for me at dinner, and always, always waited in the mornings until I got dressed, so together, we could walk to the restaurant and share a table. By the middle of our second ski weekend together, Rafe and I were a thing, and the club had no doubts about it.

Sometimes I even wondered if he had a wife. Not only did he act like he was single, but he never said a word about her, good or bad. He talked about his children, his historic house, the kitchen that he remodeled himself, his garden, his grouchy neighbor on the right who, he swore, had mental problems, his solar energy project that he was trying to install in his house, the new wing added to the side that seemed to be taking forever to finish. *Time that could be spent with me*, I lamented. And so on. But never a word about his wife. He never told me her name, never mentioned her in conversation, never delighted in telling me her evil points so that he could justify his behavior. I got to the point where I wondered if Rafe had any guilt in him at all. *He's had to have done this before*, I reasoned, as he seemed to breeze through this affair effortlessly. He knew exactly how to balance me, his emotions, his marriage. Nothing seemed to be on the rocks, not our relationship, not his marriage. I was beginning to think of him as a love machine.

But Rafe was more than that, I knew. He was a warm person, realistic in the sense that he wasn't living in a fantasy world about our relationship. He wasn't putting undue demands on me. The only thing he would interject from time to time was, "You drive me crazy."

Of course, I didn't mind hearing that. I loved every word, hung on to them each and every time. I couldn't get enough of his sweet murmurings, and oftentimes told him he was feeding me lines.

"Alright, I'm feeding you lines. Now I won't say it again."

"I'm sorry," I'd say, feeling awful about my insecurities. "I guess what you say is too good to be true."

"Then, why don't you believe me when I talk to you. Don't you think I feel this way?" His eyes were pleading with me then.

"No."

"You don't?" He seemed incredulous.

"No, not really. I want you to, and I'm glad to hear these things when you tell me. But deep down underneath, no. I guess I don't believe you."

He turned his face to the window. We were heading south on I-95 through Massachusetts on the ski bus, snowy pine trees jutting out unpredictably from the icy, snow-packed woods. We had just finished another weekend of skiing at Waterville.

"Well, Rafe, I don't know these things unless you tell me. When you do, it's always a surprise. A pleasant one, but still a surprise."

"You should know by now that I'm crazy about you." He turned to look at me, then turned back to the window. The windows were icing up, and I kept wondering what he was looking at – the white Massachusetts snow land or the ice packing up on the window.

"I know I should, but I don't unless you tell me," I said shyly.

"That's your trouble," he said, softly, but with words that sounded like a friend's. "You don't trust me. Is it just me?" he asked, turning around again to look me in the eyes. "Or is it all men or everyone?"

They were good questions. I don't think I knew myself. And I didn't answer them.

What was happening between Rafe and me wasn't

helping our image in the club. We had had some pretty juicy conversations on those bus trips, and I was sure that every word could be overheard if someone wanted to hear them.

We had finished another weekend of skiing at Waterville, and I had just decided, again, that I was madly in love with him.

15

When someone loves you, you grow in confidence and self-respect, harnessing feelings of an awakening in yourself. When you love someone back, the benefits expand even further. Not only do you awaken to yourself, but you feel that there's hope, that life is bearable after all, and that it's not all drudgery, work and responsibility.

And when you must stop loving because of external reasons, there's a loss involved. Even though your heart feels strong and is beating healthily, and you can feel the blood gushing through your body like a pump sending water from the town tower, you must say goodbye. And that hurts. It hurts because that source of happiness has to be cut off, much like an infection, or the doctor's scalpel cutting the veins and arteries during surgery. One does heal. It takes a while, and we really don't want to get over it. But, eventually, we forget. And if we're lucky, someone new comes along with whom we can start over. Loving, liking, enjoying, exploring.

But the old love never disappears. One needs only an old dress that was worn in the lover's company, or a photograph of two people kissing to awaken the senses that love has passed by. It hurts to break up, but sometimes it's a good hurt. Much like the pain involved in a good massage when the masseuse rubs an aching muscle, or when you put salve on a wound and it stings but then it heals.

Sometimes one thinks that a new love will never happen again, that the past love was THE only one. And that's not happy either. But even if lost, is it worth it to love? Is it worth the eventual pain, the aching, the knowing that these two souls will never share each other again? Or hear each other's voice, or experience new events in their lives together? It's a sad knowledge, but in time you learn to rationalize it away, like it didn't really happen, or somehow life's going to get better.

One has only to hang on.

16

One year later, our romance was dead. The mountains of Vermont and New Hampshire, Bell Telephone and a year of tingling romance finally died on us. Before it happened, I had no idea it was coming.

When I stepped onto that bus headed for Killington the following winter, I was ready for anything but death. Our death. My death. Even as I watched him rubbing her back with those doctor's hands, short fingers and chair-side manner, I told myself that he was only playing our game. "Playing it cool," as he would say. I kept rationalizing the fact that the two of them sat together as a ploy to cover up our romance. I convinced myself that Rafe cared as much as I did, but by the time we stepped off the bus six hours later, my head was spinning. Something was wrong between Rafe and me, only I hadn't yet placed what it was. *After all,* I told myself, *I had no strings on him.*

The thought that Rafe's coolness might not be a part of our game plan entered my head only after the evidence piled up high enough to cover my head like snow drifts on the sides of mountains. And when it was there, I could hardly face it. Rafe cared. I knew he did. His phone calls earlier in the week. His offer to help me find a good realtor for the townhouse I was looking to buy. Admitting he loved my birthday card saying, "Happy Birthday…only if you think of me at least three times a day." His solace during the times

I spent between boyfriends, giving up, starting over. His complete loyalty during our past ski trips when he waited for me at meal times, then skied down every single slope at my side. His reassurance to me that someday I would find a guy I loved, and my complete trust in him that he meant it.

But recently, the calls were getting sparse. When he would call, they'd only last a few minutes. This in view of the time we'd spent together only months ago: the sweet nothings we whispered into each other's ears, my talking to him while typing at work or while he worked on a patient's record, his calls in between office visits behind the nurses' backs.

Montana Monica wasn't even that attractive. He had mentioned her several times over the run of weekends we'd spent together with the club. He was always amazed at her fearless abandon on the slopes. "Monica's a daredevil," he would add at the end of any remarks he made about her.

"She's always way ahead of the guys on the expert slopes."

"Did you know she's an anthropologist?"

"Yeah, there are empty apartments in Makefield. Monica just moved into one for only $800 a month."

"Monica's the secretary of our club."

By the end of our last year, I had learned a lot about Monica. I didn't suspect anything because I never thought she was that great. Good figure, shy, glasses, short frizzy hair, drank a lot at parties, chain-smoked, a little kinky sometimes with the guys, but nice. Monica was nice. She had a good reputation with the club, and especially with Rafe. He told me one time, not that I wanted to hear it, that she "doesn't go out with married guys and I have to respect her for that." I didn't know why he mentioned that tidbit of information to me, but it didn't go down easy. In fact, I felt like second choice. At the time, I kept telling myself that I didn't care. Or that it wasn't important. I only gloated over the fact that Monica had turned down a good thing.

But there he was, Friday night on the bus, with his arm around her, smiling at me from the corner of his eye. I smiled back with half of me thinking of how well he put on the act while the other half of me wondered how he could do that in front of his lover. After a few minutes of smiles, winks, and small-time talk, I realized that he couldn't do it in front of his lover if he cared for his lover. I got up from my seat near the back, brushed through the two of them in the middle of the bus – he was leaning on the arm rest in the aisle seat – and resignedly sat in a front row seat of the bus the rest of the way to Vermont. I never looked back, never listened to their laughter (ha!), never let on to anyone that I was completely crushed. My face was red, I knew it, from the heat I felt burning up from my chest to my forehead. My lips were chapped from pursing them, the magazine pages in front of me were dog-eared and chewed off from paging over and over without reading a word. My eyes fuzzy from staring out the window at the snow-melted highway, red truck lights and the dulled frost that had built up on the inside of my window.

I was stunned. Our past year together roared through my head, images of him kissing me on our first bus trip from Killington, his waiting for me in the lobby of the lodge while I dressed for breakfast, his pulling up in the Ferrari. How could he do all these things and not care?

Maybe I'm just jealous, I told myself, the blame gradually shifting from him to me. *Maybe my bio-rhythm chart would show "sensitive" today, and tomorrow on the slopes Rafe and I will be together just like old times,* I consoled myself. But then how could he have his arm around Monica? I questioned that as the bus braked to a jarring halt.

Accident ahead. More stop and go traffic. More cigarettes smoked. Out came mine, and with that came Rulf H., the truckdriver/businessman, first generation American member of the club with whom I flirted once in a while. He sat next to me and started a conversation to which I added very little. Rulf soon got the message that I was no fun that night and left my side. I soon fell asleep, leaving Monica, Rafe and whomever else wanted to join them and all the fun they were having in the middle of the bus. I didn't care, I convinced myself, at the same time hoping he was having a lousy time. I began to hate Monica.

17

By Saturday morning, I felt better. We had arrived Friday at midnight and we had all run to bed immediately. Everyone of us was anticipating the big ski ahead. Killington was big time alright: sixty slopes, gondola lifts, double, triple, and more double chairlifts intermingled all over the mountains. There was plenty there waiting for us…we just had to sleep well so we could conquer all the slopes in two days.

As we stepped off the bus in the morning, I asked him if I could make an appointment to talk to him. He laughed and said, "Yeah, of course, where?"

I suggested the longest chairlift we could find.

"Why, what's on your mind?" he asked, almost jocular. "You got problems again?"

Problems again?

He looked at me and smiled as he hoisted his skis from the ground to his shoulders. His big white teeth glistened in the sun. His black and white streaked hair combed back straight and a curl or two flipped up behind his ear. I could always tell the back of Rafe by the hint of waves in his hair.

We walked together with Kay to the slopes, and while we fastened our boots to our skiis, I whispered back to her that I'd meet her at the top of the chairlift. She said she didn't want to ski with Rafe's group that day. I agreed.

"Not with Monica and them. They're too

competitive," she remarked.

"No, me neither, Kay. I just want to talk to him and then I'll ski with you."

"Good luck, Becca," she hollered as she walked away. She looked back at me as though she was watching me walk to the guillotine.

Rafe and I slipped up together on the chairlift, pulled the safety bar in front of us, and started our journey together.

"So, what's on your mind?" he started out, a little too casually for my predicament.

"Well, you see, Rafe, I wanted to ... I wanted to apologize for last night."

"Last night?" He looked at me with a huge question mark on his face. "What happened last night?"

"Well," I started, beginning to stammer, which I did sometimes when I got nervous. "When you were seated next to Montana Monica on the bus, I didn't want to make you uncomfortable. I just wasn't thinking."

"Don't worry about it. I wasn't uncomfortable."

Wasn't uncomfortable?

The chair approached the middle of its journey. I was running out of time. How could he be comfortable getting cozy with one gal while the other one was fuming on the same bus?

"You mean, you didn't feel uncomfortable last night?"

"No, not really," he said. "These things happen."

He looked away from me at the skiers on the slopes underneath us. "Look at that snow. We lucked out today, didn't we? Boy, what a beautiful day." He was very distracted. "Oh wait, what was your problem?" He seemed to be adding it as an after thought. "Is that what was bothering you?"

I was crushed. This wasn't turning out the way I wanted.

"Well, um, Rafe, things are getting a little sticky at the club. People are talking and I don't like it. We're being noticed."

I wasn't telling the truth. I wasn't even near saying what I wanted to say. I wanted to grab him by the throat and squeeze the blood out of his veins. Or slash his wrists and watch his blood drip onto the crispy white snow underneath our chair lift. I was that angry.

What was really on my mind was *how could you hurt me like that?*

"People are going to talk not matter what," he answered. "You wouldn't believe the gossip I've heard about myself since I starting working at the hospital. Things that I knew weren't true. That's why I don't pay attention to talk. Talk is more than cheap. It's worthless.

"Besides," he added as our lift got close to the end, "no one knows anything about us."

We were approaching the sign that said, "PREPARE FOR UNLOADING. RELEASE SAFETY BAR." I still had things on my mind to say to him that felt undone.

All the arguments for breaking up had drifted away from my mind, much like the snow that had drifted into the corners and crevices below us on the slopes.

"Have a nice day," he hollered out to me as we skied off the chair.

I skied to the right as he skied to the left, and when I got my balance, I turned around and hollered back. "You too." I was amazed at the voice that was coming out of my throat. It actually sounded normal. Kay was waiting for me over by the diagram of all the slopes on the mountains with the "YOU ARE HERE" arrow. We took off.

At the bottom of the slope, Kay and I skied over to the chairlift taking us to another ski area. I was silent, staring straight ahead of me, watching all the skiers load back onto the lift while the line gradually moved forward.

"You alright, Becca?" Her voice was low and serious and ever so gentle and tender.

"Yes, Kay," I responded, staring out at the beautiful white snow-covered trees and branches, wondering if I'd ever have a life again. "Just give me a few years and I'll be back to normal."

18

Our ending wasn't so sweet as the beginning. Late at night. End of ski trip. Exhilaration over skiing a weekend's worth of slopes. The knowledge that we all had done it again, skied miles of slopes on steep mountainsides, sometimes snowey, sometimes icy. Sore shoulders, chapped lips, calves that wouldn't stop aching, and muscles here and there that we never knew we had just waiting to be massaged. But no injuries!

He sat with Montana Monica the whole trip home. Two small cardboard buckets of ice were carted to their seats for the whiskey they would pour all the way home. Rafe's familiar blanket stuffed in the space above their heads, along with his orange Muneri ski glasses he had fastened to the boot tree laying next to his suitcase. Monica chain-smoked the whole way home, all six hours, and I thought to myself how sad that I didn't even care that he minded smoke. One less point in her favor, I would have thought at one time. Now, I just about remembered that he didn't smoke at all. Or so I told myself.

I continued to hate her.

We hadn't said a word that whole time except when I watched him carry ice out to the bus before we left the mountains of Vermont for mid-New Jersey. "Some party you're having," I mused out loud to him as we passed in opposite directions through the doorway of the Red Ribbon Lodge.

"Yeah, it's a long ride home," he answered, looking sheepish for the first time. At the same time, his eyes said, *I'm going to have a good time, dammit.*

Neither of us looked back.

Then, early that next morning, Monday morning to be exact, when the bus pulled back into the same shopping plaza in Trenton where our cars were parked in the far corner, all 40 of us scrambled for first place in line for luggage, skis and boots outside the bus. It was midnight, and we were all anxious to get home so we could sleep and then go to work later that day and not fall asleep at our desks. I found my skis and walked to the Volkswagen, unlocked the rack on the back engine lid, placed the skis there, and got back into the car and started the engine, in order to warm it up for the ride home to Walnut Hill and my mother's house. I turned on my headlights and could see Rafe's Ferrari to the right of my car. I watched him run back and forth, loading his stuff up quick.

I was very sleepy, and by this time, my brain didn't register quite the sight of Rafe ahead of me. I got back out of my car and walked over to get my suitcase. I was standing in line beside the others next to the bus. Rafe walked in front of me, turned around, and called out in the nicest voice he had, "Goodnight now. Have a safe trip home."

That was nice, I thought in my sleepiness, and I returned the compliment back to him. Somehow, I smiled, one of the best ones I could muster.

He called the next week while I was at work and apologized. I was silent for a few seconds until I could think of what to say. I came up with something that wasn't halfway near what I should have said. Maybe I should have told him off or how dare he do that to me, sit and party with another woman while I sat by myself. And all that stuff. But I knew it would only make him happier to have gotten away from a bitter woman.

"That's alright," I said, trying to think of a good response. "I guess I wanted more than I could have."

He was now quiet, and within a minute, we were off the phone.

I thought I'd never see him again, and rumor had it that he had quit our club and would then join another one the next season. He was a nice guy, they all said at the club, many times to me, and I always made sure I heartily agreed. If they intimated that we had an affair, I let it go. *After all, they can only guess,* I told myself, *and they'll never really know. Only Rafe and I know.*

Many times I thought of that last smile I gave Rafe, and the one he returned to me that night at the luggage bin on the side of the bus. I wondered back and forth whether he had really stopped caring for me, or whether I had changed. Or whether he had changed. Outgrown the relationship. I doubted it. I realized later that he wanted to roam, and I wanted him to stay, and that I was never going to get my way. He never budged from his marriage, as far as I knew, no matter how much I drove him crazy.

Mo called me early one morning at work several months later.

"Did you hear about the accident?" she asked. Her voice was cracking and serious.

"No. Whose?" I asked, wondering who in my world and Mo's would deserve such an early morning call.

"It was Rafe. He was killed in a car accident yesterday up in Hamilton Township. It was in this morning's paper."

I was stunned. And quiet. It took a while for this to register in my brain.

"I'm so sorry, Becca," she said, quietly and gently.

I couldn't get my thoughts in order at first. Then, "Mo, no. Are you sure it's THE Rafe," I whispered, hoping she had made a huge mistake.

"Well, it's got his first name and last, and Moorestown where you said he lived."

I could hear a newspaper rattling in the background of her phone. "Read it to me, Mo. Please." My voice was getting shaky. I didn't know whether to be happy or sad. I hadn't seen him in what seemed like years.

"How about if I fax it to you, Becca?" she offered.

I was again quiet, still trying to digest the fact that he was dead.

"Oh Becca. I know you've had a hard time with it. Especially since that last ski trip."

I didn't know what to say to her. She was so good

about not admonishing me for the whole affair. Yet, Mo had her scruples and had a good sense of fairness and justice and mercy and compassion. She never judged me right or wrong. In his presence, she was always nice and didn't let on that she knew anything. I guess she figured the whole thing would run its course. And it had.

I started crying. Right at my desk. At work.

"Do you want me to fax this article to you," she asked as gently as she could muster. I said yes, and in between muffled cries, I gave her the number.

I ran into the fax room as it blew out of the machine. I grabbed the sheet, practically mid-air, and ran into the ladies' room quickly. There, in a somewhat lengthy article, were the details of the crash. Two people killed. One was the driver. And the other? A woman who was sitting in the front seat of the Ferrari had also died. The crash was ugly. And sudden. Apparently speed was a factor. And late at night.

Mo didn't give me a follow up of the story in the papers. She failed to mentioned who it was that died with him, mainly because I refused to ask her. I don't think I could have handled knowing who it was. On the one hand, I wished it were his wife. That's who should have been in that car with him. But I suspected it wasn't. On the other, someone had to raise the kids.

I also didn't want it to be Monica who died or any other woman of importance to him. But then I never did get my final wishes with Rafe.

I was sorry he died. He didn't quite deserve that. He certainly had a huge impact on my life. He conversed with me and had insights into my psyche like no man ever did. And for that, I'll always love him.

I didn't cry again over Rafe's death for several weeks. I vacillated over whether to be happy or sad. He had brought me so much happiness. And so much pain. I asked myself, *which most do I remember him by?* He will always be a part of me, no matter what. No matter about his marriage, his kids, Montana Monica, and whomever else he wished to be with before, during or after me.

As much as it had to end with us, I was not sorry it did. I wished so much we didn't have obstacles in our way. I just couldn't surmount them. It wasn't in my blood. It was in his. He wanted to have a good time – I wanted stability and trust and a good and faithful lover. I was a one-man-at-a-time type of woman, in spite of everything that happened while I knew him. He, according to my knowledge of him, wanted to play. And so he did. Many times I wished I could play with him, but I couldn't. At least not for the long run.

I didn't want to find out what had gone on with Monica, if anything. But I made a promise to myself then, that I would give it considerable thought while I am sitting in a rocking chair in some nursing home, reminiscing, hopefully a long, long time from now. My hatred for her gradually dissipated. Until one day months later, I called Mo.

"Who died in the car with Rafe? I have to know."

"It was Monica," she said.

"Bless me father, for I have sinned." I could hear the priest on the other side of the wooden panel shuffle his feet as I pressed my knees down on the kneeler and made the sign of the cross with my right hand.

"Father, I had an affair with a married man." It was almost two years after Rafe's death that I was finally able to ask God for forgiveness.

"And why, my child of God," he asked after a too-long silence, in a hushed but somewhat stern voice, "did you commit such a sin? Especially since, I presume, you knew he was already married?"

My face was red hot with humiliation and embarrassment. *I don't know why I did it*, I thought to myself. *But I'd better come up with something if I want this representative of Christ to absolve me of my sins.*

"I'm not sure yet, Father," I stammered, in a very low and contrite voice. "I think I was lonely."

Silence on the other end. A long pause, almost like a knowing pause. *Who more than a priest could know loneliness*, I pondered.

I started to sweat, even though it was the dead of winter, and there was snow on the ground, and the confessional was cold. It wasn't easy asking for God's forgiveness. I had hardly forgiven myself, even two years later.

"But you know, Father," I added. "The experience

caused me a lot of pain too." I was hoping that this would count for something in the forgiveness department.

There, I said it. I was talking to the priest as though he were my best friend instead of a very powerful person who could make the difference between my future in heaven or hell.

He waited for what seemed like an eternity in itself. I suspected but didn't truly know if he was relating to the loneliness department. All kinds of thoughts ran through my head. *Had he ever skiied? Had he ever fallen in love? Had he ever been lonely, and does he know how devastating it can be?*

My little cubicle with only the kneeler in it was closing in on me, and becoming, dare I say it, hot as hell. I thought I had died and got sent there.

And then... "For your penance, say a full decade of the rosary."

I drew a deep breath, and said my prayer, "Oh my God, I am heartily sorry for having offended thee. And I detest all my sins, because I fear the loss of heaven and the pain of hell. But most of all, because I have offended thee, My God..." I finished my prayer of contrition and left.

I could hear the priest close the wooden panel on my side of the confessional and open the one on the other side.

Now I was free. I knew deep in my heart that God had forgiven me. After all, I was young and stupid as they would say. And lonely.

While in the confessional, the priest told me to never do it again. "Do you promise God?" he had asked.

"Yes, I do, Father," I responded.

After all the pain I had been through, it was an easy promise to keep.